BIG CITY OTTO
WRITTEN BY BILL SLAVIN
WITH ESPERANÇA MELO
ART BY BILL SLAVIN
ELEPHANTS NEVER FORGET 1
KIDS CAN PRESS

IT'S SAID THAT ELEPHANTS NEVER FORGET ...

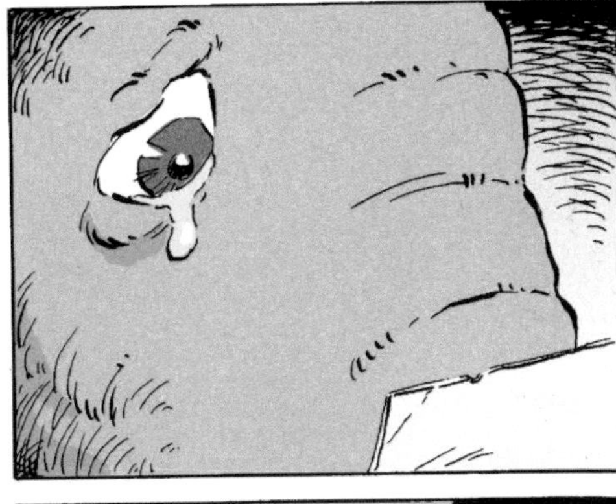
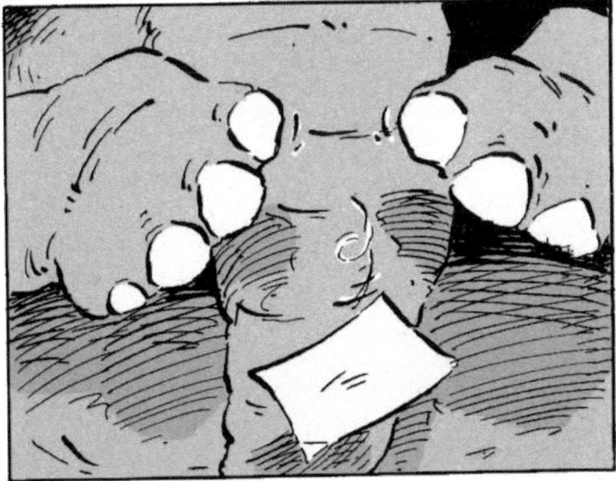

FOR OTTO'S SAKE, I
WISH THEY COULD.

POOR KID ...
OTTO! OTTO! YOU DROPPED THIS!
I KNOW I DROPPED IT. SNIFF! I DON'T WANT IT ANYMORE.
DON'T WANT IT? THE ONLY MEMENTO OF YOUR CHILDHOOD CHUM? YOU GUYS WERE LIKE BROTHERS!
BUT HE'S HERE I MY HEAD ALL TH TIME, CRACKERS AND I JUST CAN' GET HIM OUT!
TAP! TAP!

THEY WERE GOOD TIMES, OTTO, BUT GEORGIE'S GONE! YOU'VE GOTTA GET USED TO IT.
BUT I MISS HIM, CRACKERS! WE WERE PALS! AND THAT DAY STILL HAUNTS ME. I JUST FEEL I COULD HAVE DONE MORE.
ALL RIGHT. SO YOU'VE GOTTA WORK THIS THROUGH. LET'S GO OVER IT ALL AGAIN.
THE LAST YOU SAW GEORGIE HE WAS IN A SACK, AND THE MAN WITH THE WOODEN NOSE WAS ROWING AWAY WITH HIM, RIGHT?
YES! GEORGIE'S LITTLE SMILEY FACE STICKING OUT ... SOB!
C'MON, PULL YOURSELF TOGETHER! AND AFTER THAT?
SNIFF! HE TOOK HIM ON A BIG FLOATY THING.
PARP!

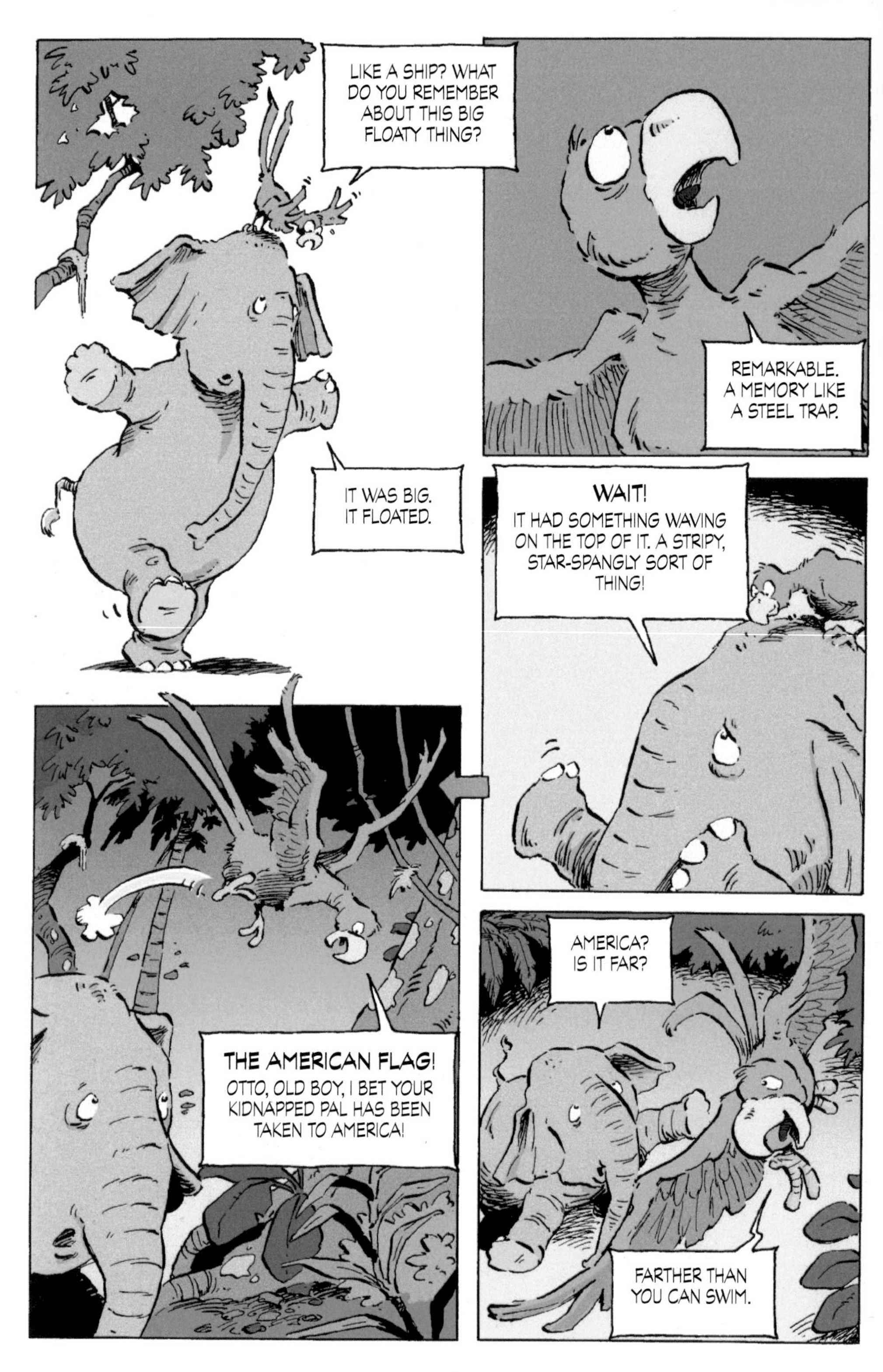
LIKE A SHIP? WHAT DO YOU REMEMBER ABOUT THIS BIG FLOATY THING?
REMARKABLE. A MEMORY LIKE A STEEL TRAP.
IT WAS BIG. IT FLOATED.
WAIT! IT HAD SOMETHING WAVING ON THE TOP OF IT. A STRIPY, STAR-SPANGLY SORT OF THING!
THE AMERICAN FLAG! OTTO, OLD BOY, I BET YOUR KIDNAPPED PAL HAS BEEN TAKEN TO AMERICA!
AMERICA? IS IT FAR?
FARTHER THAN YOU CAN SWIM.

SO IF I WANT TO FIND GEORGIE I'LL NEED A BIG FLOATY THING?
NOT ANYMORE, BIG BOY. THIS IS THE AGE OF MIRACLES. E-MAILS, TEXT MESSAGING, THINGS ZAPPED AROUND THE WORLD!
I'M NOT SURE I LIKE THE SOUND OF THAT!
NOT THINGS YOUR SIZE. BUT PEOPLE ARE A LOT SMARTER NOW. THEY FLY!

A LITTLE WHILE LATER ...
I'M GLAD YOU'RE COMING WITH ME, CRACKERS, BUT WOULDN'T THE BIG FLOATY THING BE A BETTER IDEA? THOSE METAL BIRDS LOOK KINDA FLIMSY.
IT'LL BE FINE. LET'S GO!

WE'LL HAVE TO ASK AROUND FOR DIRECTIONS.

EXCUSE ME ...
EXCUSE ME ...

COULD YOU TELL ME – ?
WE WERE WONDERING – ?

I WANT TO GO TO AMERICA!

LAND OF THE FREE AND THE BRAVE? GATE 13. SHOW YOUR TICKET AND PASSPORT AT SECURITY FIRST. NO BOTTLES, NO TOENAIL CLIPPERS, NO GELS. ENJOY YOUR TRIP!
?
TICKET? PASSPORT? SECURITY? THIS MIGHT BE TRICKIER THAN WE THOUGHT ...
CHECK-IN
IT'S TOO BIG. YOU'LL HAVE TO TAKE IT TO SPECIAL AND OVERSIZED BAGGAGE!
SPECIAL? OVERSIZED? THAT'S YOU, OTTO!
3

SPECIAL AND OVERSIZED BAGGAGE
WRAP UP THAT PARCEL FOR SHIPPING, WILL YOU?
WHICH PARCEL?

THE BIG UGLY THING WITH THE TRUNK. AND THEN GET IT LOADED. I'M GOING FOR COFFEE.

?!
WHIRR!
BAGGAGE WRAP

THIS IS INCREDIBLE LUCK. JUST ACT LIKE YOU'RE STUFFED.
ACTUALLY, I'M A BIT PECKISH!

CRACKERS?
YEAH?
DO YOU THINK I'M UGLY?
CLUNK!

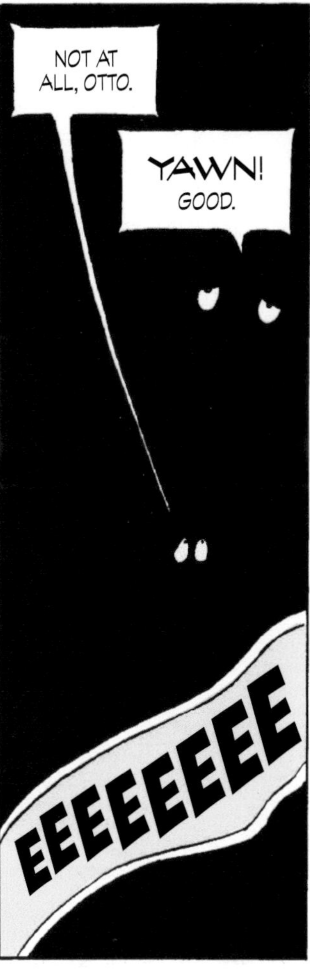
NOT AT ALL, OTTO.
YAWN! GOOD.
EEEEEEEE

ZZZZ!
G'NIGHT, OTTO.
VROOOM!

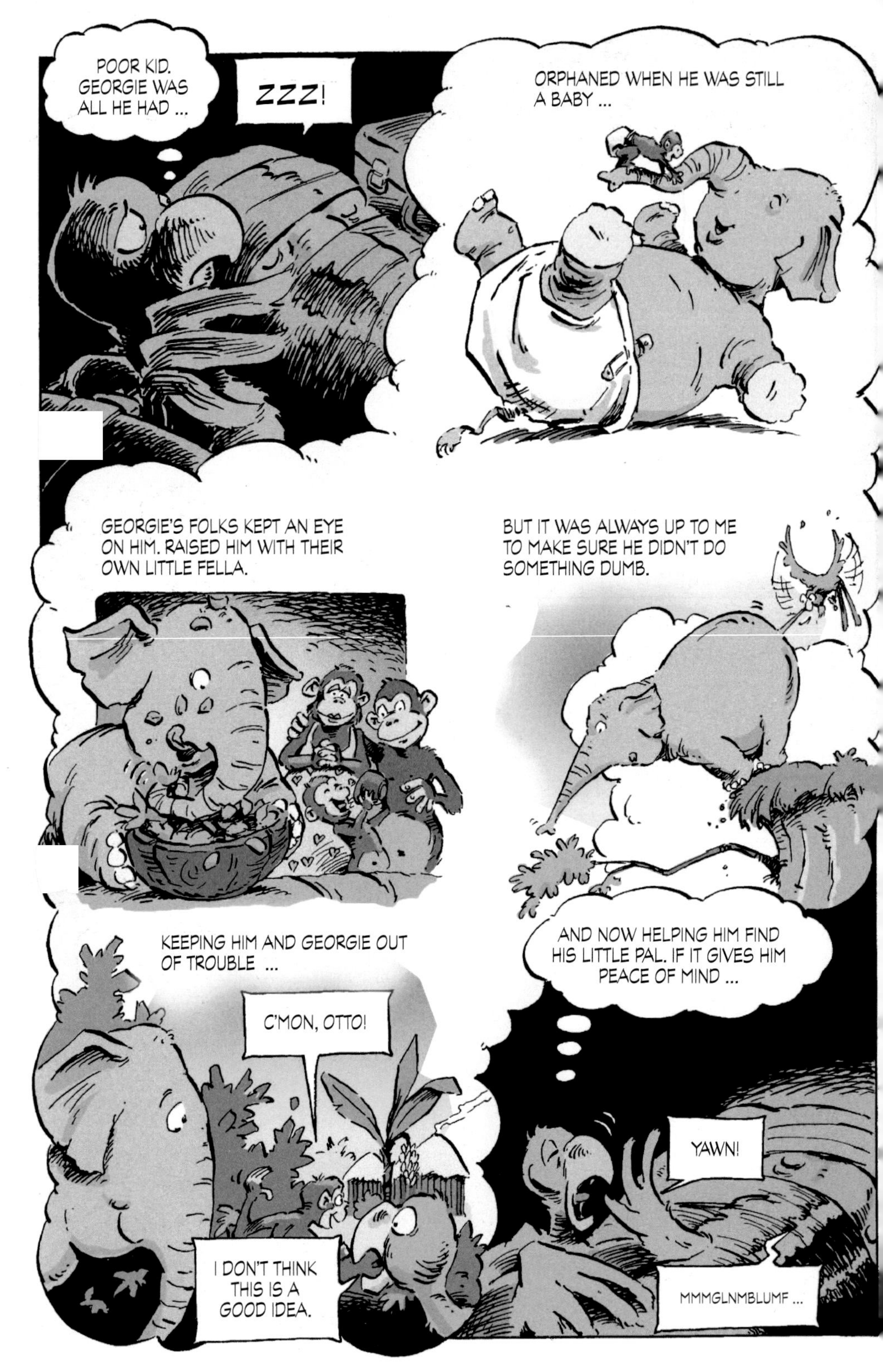
POOR KID. GEORGIE WAS ALL HE HAD ...
ZZZ!
ORPHANED WHEN HE WAS STILL A BABY ...
GEORGIE'S FOLKS KEPT AN EYE ON HIM. RAISED HIM WITH THEIR OWN LITTLE FELLA.
BUT IT WAS ALWAYS UP TO ME TO MAKE SURE HE DIDN'T DO SOMETHING DUMB.
KEEPING HIM AND GEORGIE OUT OF TROUBLE ...
C'MON, OTTO!
I DON'T THINK THIS IS A GOOD IDEA.
AND NOW HELPING HIM FIND HIS LITTLE PAL. IF IT GIVES HIM PEACE OF MIND ...
YAWN!
MMMGLNMBLUMF ...

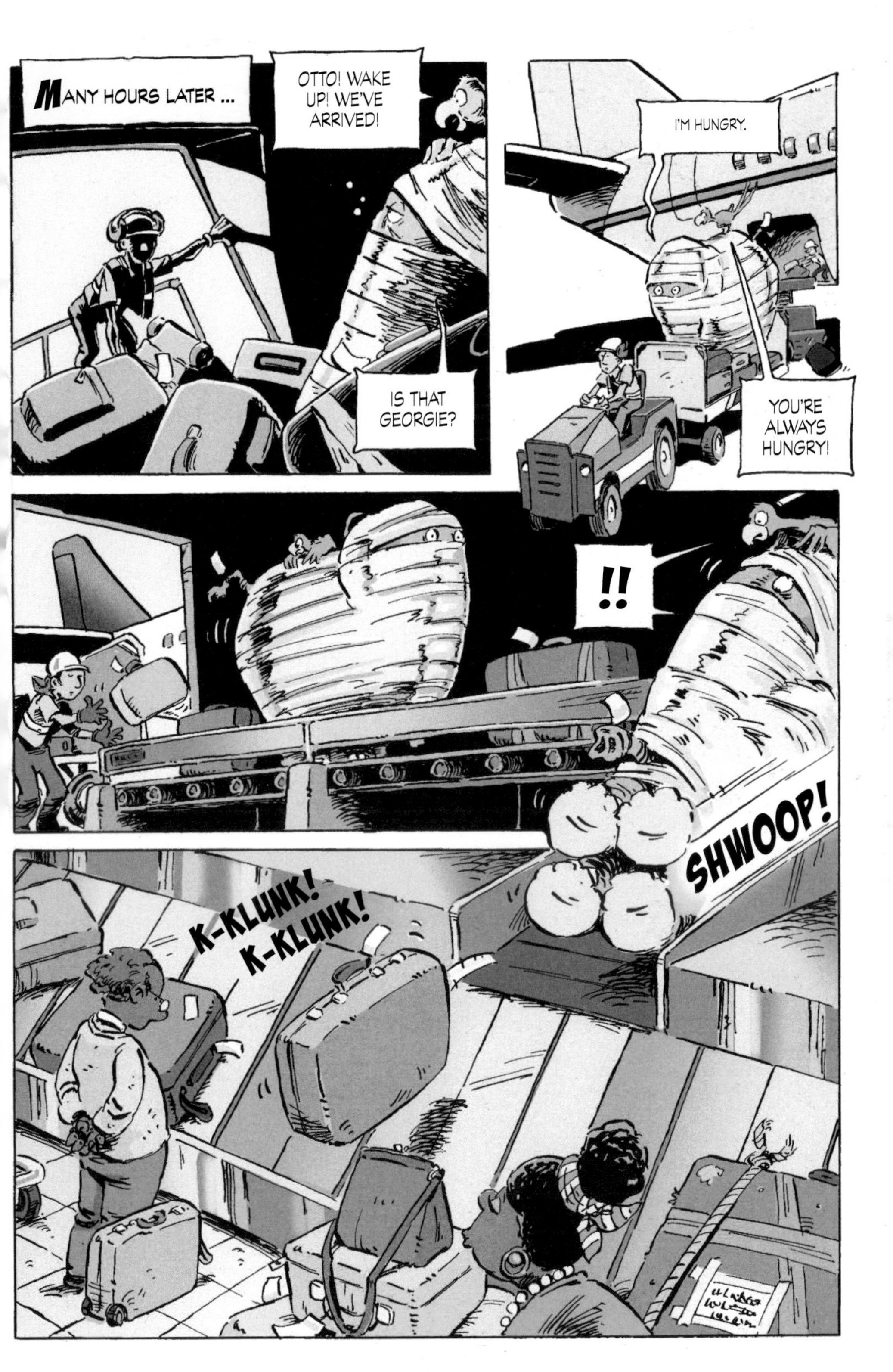
MANY HOURS LATER ...
OTTO! WAKE UP! WE'VE ARRIVED!
IS THAT GEORGIE?
I'M HUNGRY.
YOU'RE ALWAYS HUNGRY!
!!
SHWOOP!
K-KLUNK! K-KLUNK!

LOST BAGGAGE
JUST STAY PUT UNTIL EVERYONE GOES!
K-KLUNK! K-KLUNK!
E2
A LITTLE LATER ...
LOST BAGGAGE
... ABOUT THIS BIG, BUMPY, BIG TEETH ...
K-KLUNK! K-KLUNK!
E2
MUCH LATER ...
LOST BAGGAGE
I'M SO HUNGRY I COULD EAT A PEANUT!
DON'T EVEN JOKE, OTTO. YOU KNOW YOU AND PEANUTS. JUST A BIT LONGER.
K-KLUNK! K-KLUNK!
E2

MUCH, MUCH LATER ...
GNNNNGH!
FINALLY! THE AIRPORT'S SHUT DOWN. NOW TO FIND OUR WAY OUT OF HERE!
POP!
WAIT!

THIS IS AMERICA. YOU CAN'T GO AROUND LOOKING, ER ...
OVERSIZED? SPECIAL?
EXACTLY!

HERE. TRY SOME OF THESE.
?!

HMM ... TOO OBVIOUS.
I'M WITH STUPID
I DON'T LIKE THE INSINUATION.
NOW THAT'S JUST A CRY FOR HELP! JIMINY, WHAT WOULD YOU DO WITHOUT ME? TRY THESE.
PERFECT. INCOGNITO!

?
YIKES! WE'RE A LONG WAY OUT OF TOWN.

IT'S TOO LATE TO CATCH A CAB ...

AND THE DOORS ARE LOCKED! SHEESH!
RATTLE! RATTLE!

HOW THE HECK ARE WE GOING TO GET OUT OF HERE?
TAP! TAP!

GANG WAYYY!!
?!

WHOOSH!

CRAASH!!

SURE. WE COULD DO IT LIKE THAT.

HEY, OTTO. I THINK YOU JUST SOLVED OUR TRANSPORTATION PROBLEM, TOO!
GO LEFT! NO, RIGHT! RIGHT!
ARE YOU CRAZY?!
SCREECH!
HONK!
ANIMALS!

NOT LONG AFTERWARD ...
LOOK, FRUIT!
I'M NOT SURE WE CAN TAKE THOSE, OTTO ...
EASY THERE, FELLA. THAT'S A LOT OF PRUNES.
AH, THAT'S BETTER.
NOT BAD. ALTHOUGH I WAS REALLY IN THE MOOD FOR A CRACKER.
?!
RUMBLE!
RUMBLE!

AROOOOOOOOOOOOOOOOO
WE'VE GOT A 269 UP AT THE AIRPORT.
10-4.
WE'RE ON OUR WAY.
SO WHERE DO WE START LOOKING FOR GEORGIE?
JUST ASK AROUND, I GUESS. I MEAN, HOW MANY PEOPLE CAN ACTUALLY LIVE HERE?
EXCUSE ME ...
WE'RE LOOKING FOR A GUY NAMED GEORGIE ...

THE NAME'S GEORGIE. CUTE LITTLE GUY. ABOUT THIS TALL ...
COULD YOU TELL ME – ?

COULD YOU HELP US, PLEASE?
IS ANYONE OUT THERE LISTENING??!!
MEANWHILE, AT THE AIRPORT ...
SO WADDAYA GOT?
LOOKS LIKE AN INSIDE JOB – LUGGAGE VANDALIZED, BREAK AND EXIT.
AND A BIT OF VIDEO. A BIG FAT GUY AND A LITTLE SQUIRT.

BACK ON THE STREET ...
LET'S FOLLOW THOSE PEOPLE. THEY SEEM TO KNOW WHERE THEY'RE GOING!
THIS IS HOPELESS.
SUBWAY
ZZZZ ...
Visit the ZOO!
ZZZZ ...
ZZZZ ...
CLICKETY-CLICK! CLICKETY-CLICK!
OH, CRACKERS, THAT LOOKS LIKE FUN!
WHAT LOOKS LIKE FUN?
THE CLICKETY-CLICK MACHINE. CAN I GIVE IT A WHIRL?

OH, BOY!
FUN? WHA – ? OTTO, WHAT COULD POSSIBLY BE FUN ABOUT GOING THROUGH A TURNSTILE?
CLICKETY-CLICK! CLICKETY-CLICK!

WELL, LOOK AT ALL THESE PEOPLE! WHY ELSE WOULD THEY LINE UP?
URRRGH!
CLICKETY-CLICK! CLICKETY-CLICK!

ZZZZZ – ?
CLICKETY-CLUNK!

HEY! I'M STUCK!
YOU NEED MONEY. AND BESIDES, YOU'RE TOO –

!!
YES?
UH-OH! RUN FOR IT, OTTO!

CRASH!
STOP!
WHY DO YOU ALWAYS HAVE TO BREAK THINGS?
WHY IS EVERYTHING MADE SO SMALL? IT'S SIZISM!
NORTHBOUND PLATFORM
I THINK WE GAVE HIM THE SLIP!
EEEEK!
YIKES! WHAT NOW?!
OH, NO!

THE TRAIN'S COMING!
MY BABEEEE!
GURGLE GOOGOO!

I'LL GET 'IM.
HOOT! HOOT!
OTTO!

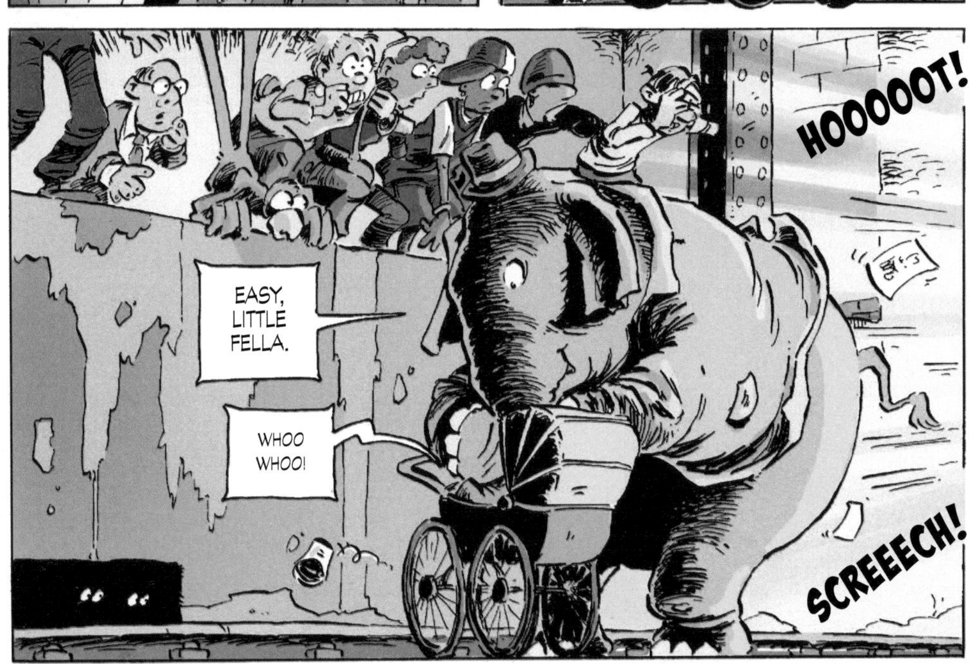
HOOOOOT!
EASY, LITTLE FELLA.
WHOO WHOO!
SCREEECH!

BUMP!

YOU REALLY SHOULD BE MORE CAREFUL. THAT FALL MIGHT HAVE HURT HIM!
HOORAY!
CLAP!
CLAP!
CLAP!
WHA – ? WHAT'S UP?
NEVER MIND, BIG GUY.
UH-OH, OTTO, TROUBLE'S BACK!

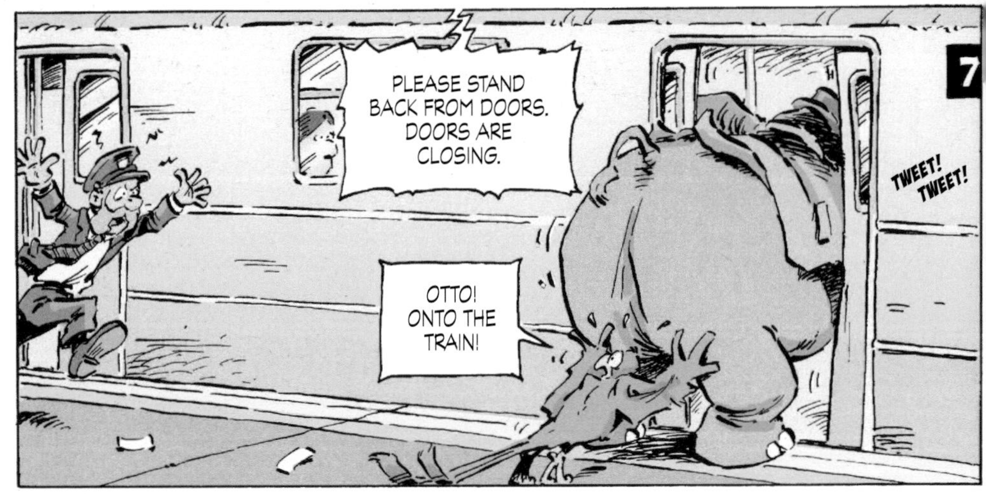
PLEASE STAND BACK FROM DOORS. DOORS ARE CLOSING.
TWEET! TWEET!
OTTO! ONTO THE TRAIN!

SHHHHHK!

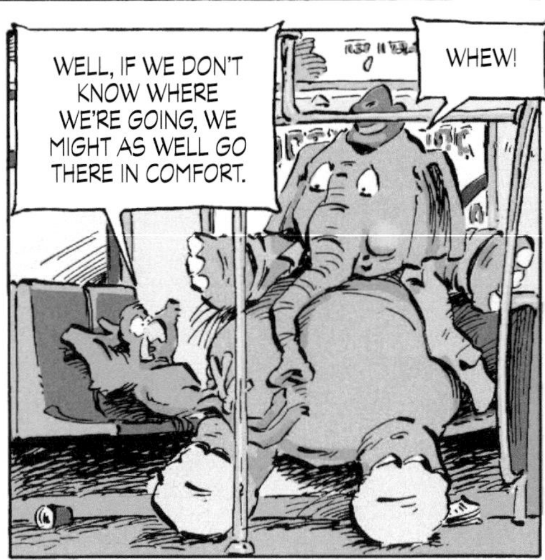
WELL, IF WE DON'T KNOW WHERE WE'RE GOING, WE MIGHT AS WELL GO THERE IN COMFORT.
WHEW!

WHOOOOOSH!

A FEW STOPS LATER ...
SHHHHHK!
7269
WHERE DO ALL THESE PEOPLE COME FROM?
CRACKERS! LOOK! IT'S THE MAN WITH THE WOODEN NOSE!
QUICK! LET'S GET HIM!
CAREFUL, OTTO. SEE THAT CASE HE'S CARRYING? IT MIGHT HOLD A WEAPON.
OTTO, WE NEED A PLAN!
YOU TRIP HIM AND I'LL SIT ON HIM!
THAT'S A PLAN?!

GEROMINO!
SWOOSH!

OOF!
WHUMP!

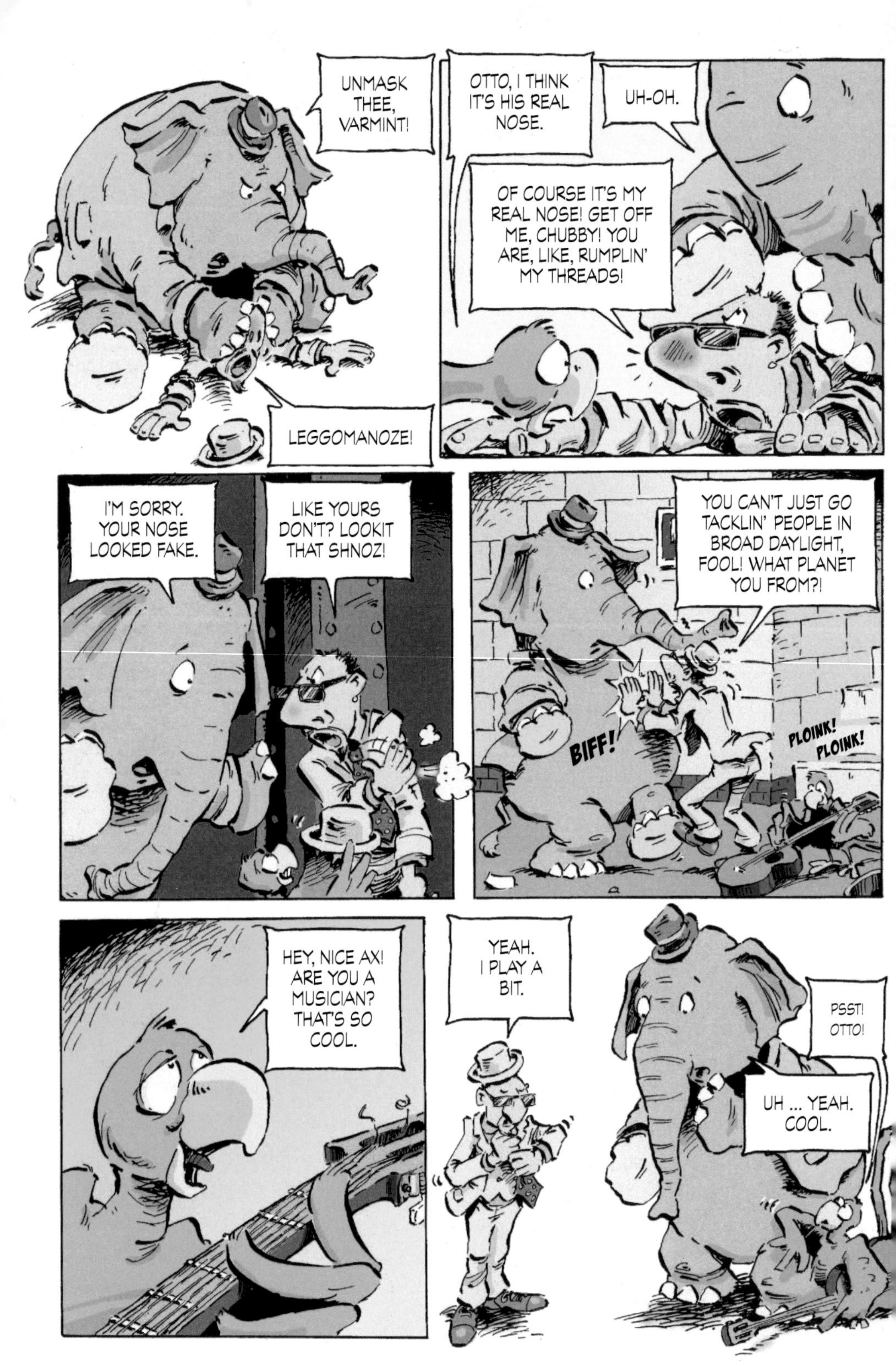
UNMASK THEE, VARMINT!
LEGGOMANOZE!
OTTO, I THINK IT'S HIS REAL NOSE.
UH-OH.
OF COURSE IT'S MY REAL NOSE! GET OFF ME, CHUBBY! YOU ARE, LIKE, RUMPLIN' MY THREADS!
I'M SORRY. YOUR NOSE LOOKED FAKE.
LIKE YOURS DON'T? LOOKIT THAT SHNOZ!
YOU CAN'T JUST GO TACKLIN' PEOPLE IN BROAD DAYLIGHT, FOOL! WHAT PLANET YOU FROM?!
BIFF!
PLOINK!
PLOINK!
HEY, NICE AX! ARE YOU A MUSICIAN? THAT'S SO COOL.
YEAH. I PLAY A BIT.
PSST! OTTO!
UH ... YEAH. COOL.

MAYBE YOU'VE CAUGHT MY ACT? I PLAY AT GEORGIE'S.
?!

GEORGIE? YOU KNOW GEORGIE??
SURE. EVERYONE KNOWS GEORGIE. JUST AROUND THE CORNER, MAN.

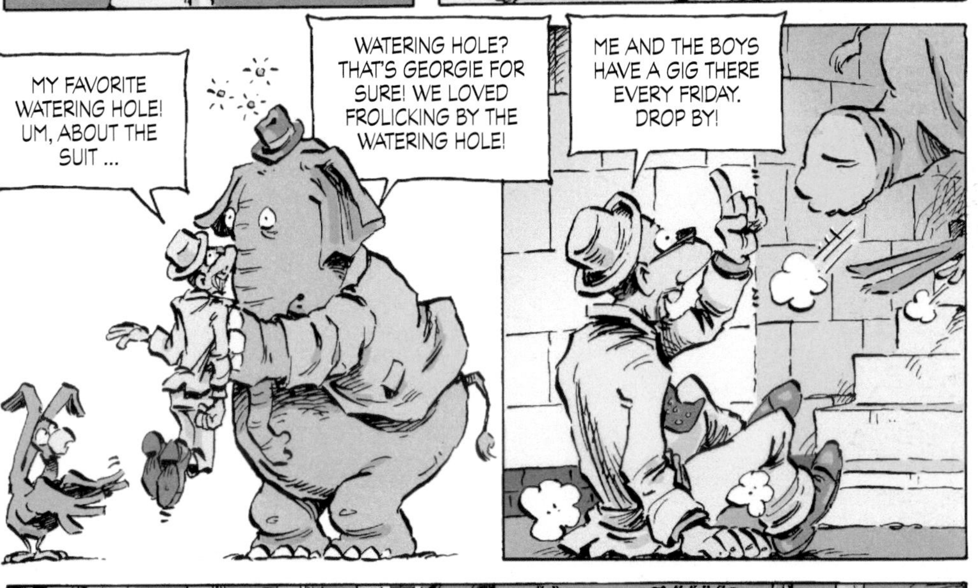

MY FAVORITE WATERING HOLE! UM, ABOUT THE SUIT ...
WATERING HOLE? THAT'S GEORGIE FOR SURE! WE LOVED FROLICKING BY THE WATERING HOLE!
ME AND THE BOYS HAVE A GIG THERE EVERY FRIDAY. DROP BY!

Georgie's

Georgie
FUNNY LOOKING WATERING HOLE.

MANGO JUICE, STRAIGHT UP!
DITTO. AND CAN I GET MINE WITH ONE OF THOSE LITTLE UMBRELLAS?
SURE, HONEY.

YOU KNOW WHAT WOULD FANCY THIS PLACE UP? PALM TREES.

SO WE'RE LOOKING FOR GEORGIE.
YOU'RE NOT GEORGIE.
I'M GEORGIE.

DIDN'T YOU SEE THE SIGN OUTSIDE?
I THINK SHE'S A DIFFERENT GEORGIE.
WHAT IS IT WITH THIS CITY?! GEORGIES ON EVERY CORNER! WATERING HOLES WITH NO PALM TREES!
I'M NEVER GOING TO SEE GEORGIE AGAIN!
BOO HOO HOO!
A GIRL, HUH?
NOPE. A CHIMP.
HEY, BIG FELLA. IT'S GONNA BE ALL RIGHT. YOU'LL FIND YOUR PAL. HERE, HAVE ANOTHER MANGO JUICE – ON THE HOUSE.
SOB!
SNIFF! THANKS.
SLURP!
?!
IT'S BEEN A ROUGH MORNING.
SNIFF!
C'MON, OTTO. LET'S HIT THE PAVEMENT.
GOOD LUCK!

HOURS LATER ...
CRIPES! WE'VE BEEN SEARCHING FOR AGES!
I GOTTA GO.
AIRPORT VANDALS
POK!
GO? NOW? WE JUST FLEW 3000 MILES TO GET HERE AND YOU GOTTA GO?!
NO, I MEAN GO! YOU KNOW ...
AH, JEEZ! THIS AIN'T THE JUNGLE, OTTO. YOU CAN'T JUST GO ANYWHERE.

SEE THAT LITTLE HOUSE? YOU GO THERE.
♫
ZIP!
IT SEEMS A BIT SMALL ...

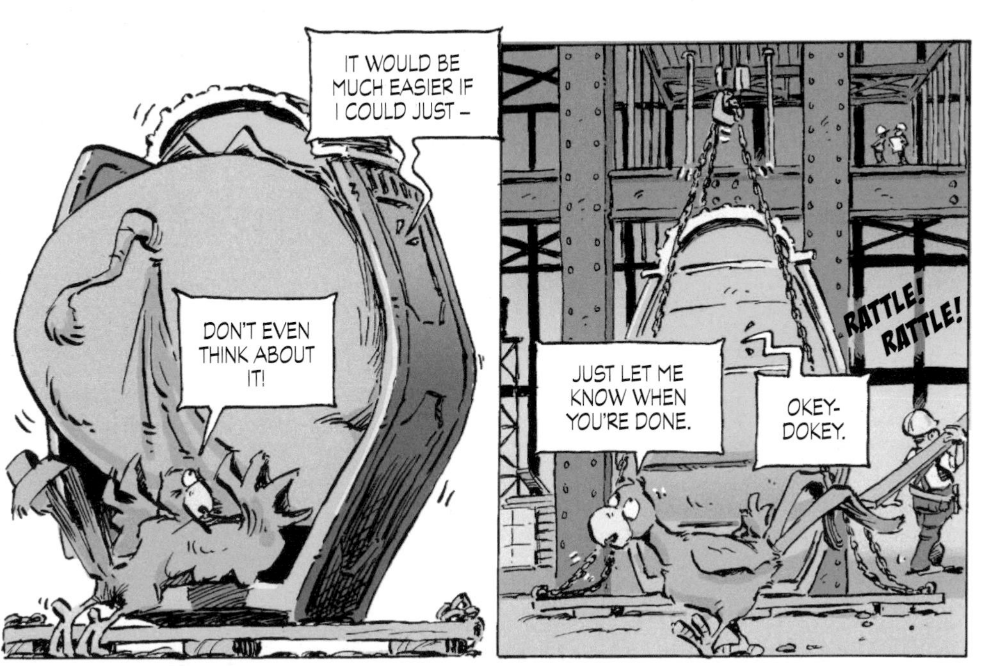
IT WOULD BE MUCH EASIER IF I COULD JUST –
DON'T EVEN THINK ABOUT IT!
RATTLE! RATTLE!
JUST LET ME KNOW WHEN YOU'RE DONE.
OKEY-DOKEY.

I'M FEELING MUCH LIGHTER.
JUST HURRY UP, WOULD YA?
TAP! TAP!

I TOLD YOU NOT TO EAT ALL THOSE –
WHAA – ?!!

OTTO!

OTTO! OTTO!
I'M COMING! JUST A MINUTE!
NO, OTTO! THIS IS BAD! YOU GOTTA GET OUTTA THERE!
FLUSH!
SO WHAT'S THE –
EEEEEK!

AIEEE!

STEADY, BIG BOY. STEADY. JUST MAKE YOUR WAY OVER TO THE MIDDLE HERE ...

IT'S HUGE! LIKE A MASSIVE JUNGLE, BUT MADE OUT OF ... UMM ...
CONCRETE?
SNIFF! WE'RE NEVER GOING TO FIND GEORGIE, ARE WE, CRACKERS?
SURE WE WILL, BIG BUDDY.

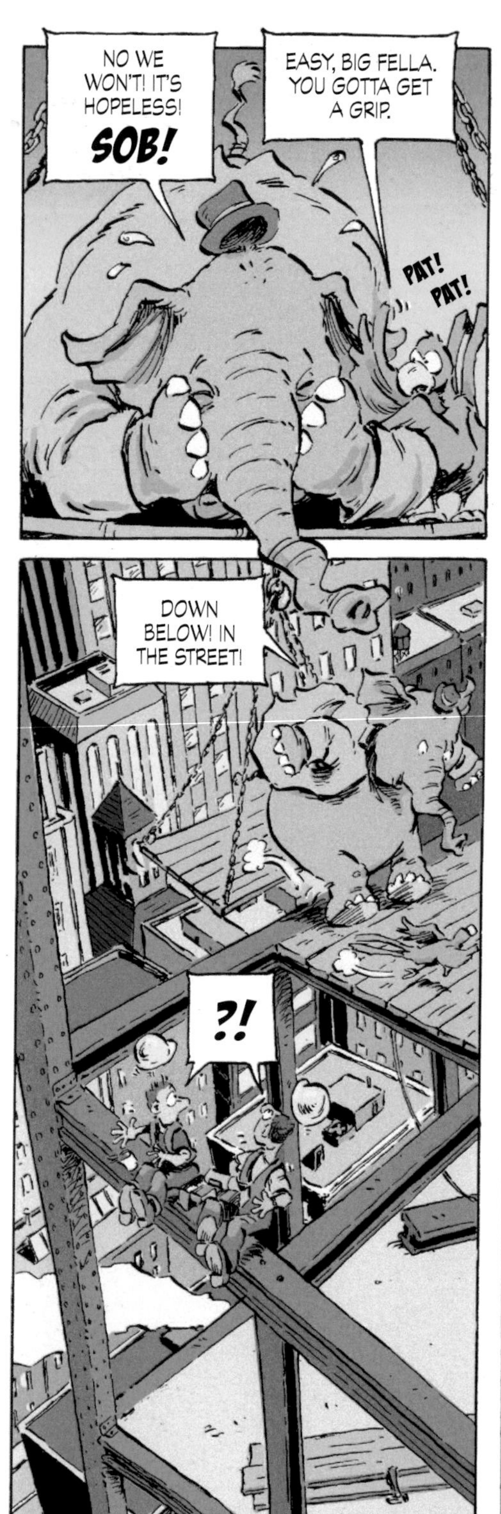
NO WE WON'T! IT'S HOPELESS! SOB!
EASY, BIG FELLA. YOU GOTTA GET A GRIP.
PAT! PAT!
DOWN BELOW! IN THE STREET!
?!

WAIT! I SEE HIM! THERE!
WHERE?!

I'M SURE IT WAS HIM!

GEORGIE!!
?!
OH, GEORGIE! HAS IT COME TO THIS? BEGGING FOR YOUR SUPPER?
ER ... OTTO. I DON'T THINK IT'S GEORGIE.
PLEASE, SIR, UNHAND MY MONKEY!
YOU'RE NOT GEORGIE!
BEAT IT, JUMBO. YA BLOCKIN' MY SUN!
YOU'RE RIGHT, CRACKERS. HE ISN'T GEORGIE. HE'S MUCH RUDER THAN GEORGIE.
THUNK!

AND GEORGIE IS ... ?
A LITTLE CHIMP. LIKE YOU. ONLY CUTER.
LISTEN, BUD! I DON'T KNOW WHO YOU ARE OR WHEN YOU GOT OFF DA BOAT, BUT I'M NOT A CHIMP.
I'M A MONKEY. M-O-N-K-E-Y! JUST 'CAUSE YOU CAN'T TELL THE DIFFERENCE 'TWEEN ME AND YER PRECIOUS LITTLE PAL ...
WELL, IT'S JUST BECAUSE YOU'RE A MONKEY, HE'S A CHIMP –
AND YOU'RE A CHUMP! US BOTH BEING PRIMATES DON'T MAKE HIM MY COUSIN! I WAS BORN ON THE 4TH OF JULY! I'M AMERICAN!
LISTEN, WE DIDN'T MEAN TO OFFEND ...
IT'S THE SAME THING, DAY IN, DAY OUT. "WHERE YOU FROM, CUTE LITTLE FELLA?" "MOMMA, LOOK AT THE BABY CHIMPANZEE!"
SNIFF! IT'S JUST THAT WE'VE BEEN LOOKING ALL DAY AND EVERYONE HERE HAS BIG, FAKE-LOOKING NOSES AND IS CALLED GEORGIE ...
?!
... AND I ALMOST FELL TEN STORIES OUT OF A TOILET AND –
SOB!
JIMINY CRICKET! NOW LOOK WHAT YOU GOT STARTED!
AWRIGHT! AWRIGHT! APOLOGY ACCEPTED.

... AND I ATE TOO MANY PRUNES, AND NOW I'M HUNGRY AGAIN, AND –
CRIPES, CAN YOU GET HIM TO STOP BLUBBERING? HE'S KILLIN' DA BUSINESS!
HE'S JUST A BIT SENSITIVE.

I'LL SAY! LISTEN, I'M DONE MY SHIFT ANYWAY. C'MON BACK TO DA CAMP AND GRAB A BITE.

THE NAME'S DJANGO. WHERE YOU FELLAS FROM? KANSAS?
A SHORT WHILE LATER ...
WELCOME TO MY HOME!

HERE! EAT!

SHLURP!

ERF! THANK YOU! IT'S – ERF – DELICIOUS!
GOOD! I LIKE A MAN WITH AN APPETITE! HAVE MORE!

... SO THAT'S WHERE WE'RE AT. JUST DEAD ENDS.
SHNAFFLE!
GLURP!
WELL, DA WAY I SEE IT, YA GOTTA TALK TO SOME OF YOUR OWN, RIGHT?

OTHERS LIKE YOU, WHO'VE COME FROM BEYOND DA BRIDGE! THEY MIGHT HAVE A TAG ON YER FRIEND.
YOU KNOW WHERE WE CAN FIND OTHER WILD ANIMALS? HERE, IN THE CITY?
SURE. IT'S A PLACE CALLED DA "ZOO"! ALMOST ALL THE FOREIGNERS GO THERE. IF YA GO NOW, YA'LL HAVE THE PLACE TO YOURSELF!

ACROSS TOWN ...
NOPE, NOPE AND NOPE.
7'0"
6'6"
6'0"

LISTEN, MAN. I TELL YA, THIS GUY WAS SUPER FAT! WITH A FREAKY LARGE NOSE AND EARS OUT TO HERE!

I MEAN, ARE YOU SURE THIS CAT'S YOUR MAN?

POLICE
THEY SEEMED SO COOL. DUG MY MUSIC! CRIMINALS?! SHEESH!

MAY I?
AFTER YOU, OLD BOY.

CRASH!

IT'S A PRISON! THEY LOCK ANIMALS UP HERE!
OH, NO. IT'S MUCH BETTER THAN THAT!

THREE MEALS A DAY, DON'T YOU KNOW? VERY FAST, VERY CONVENIENT.
?!
NO LONG LINE-UPS AT THE WATERING HOLE.
HIGHLY SANITARY!

ARE YOU ALL NUTS? LOOK AT YOU!
YOU'RE BEHIND BARS.
AND SO SHOULD YOU BE ...
YOU LOOK LIKE YOU COULD USE A DIET. THEY HAVE KEEPERS TO SET THAT UP, YOU KNOW. SLIM YOU RIGHT DOWN!

ACTUALLY, WE'RE LOOKING FOR MY FRIEND. HIS NAME'S GEORGIE. HE'S A CHIMP.
GEORGIE? DON'T RING A BELL. YOU COULD ASK AT THE MONKEY HOUSE ...

DOES ANYONE HERE KNOW A CHIMP CALLED GEORGIE?!
NOPE.
CAN'T SAY I DO.
THERE'S A HIPPO CALLED PORGIE.

WELL, DOES ANYONE KNOW OF THE MAN WITH THE WOODEN NOSE?
THE MAN WITH THE WOODEN NOSE??!!

?!

THAT WENT WELL.
DON'T WORRY ABOUT THEM.
THEY'RE A BUNCH OF FRUITCAKES. A BIT RATTLED UP HERE, KNOW WHAT I MEAN?

ME? I'D BE OUT IN A SECOND. MAYBE MAKE A SNACK OUT OF YOU TWO. HA HA!

ER ... WE WERE TOLD TO COME HERE. THAT WE MIGHT FIND HELP.
THIS CROWD WON'T BE MUCH HELP. THEY'VE FORGOTTEN WHAT IT IS TO BE ALIVE, TO BE FREE!

SO WHY ARE YOU SO INTERESTED IN THE MAN WITH THE WOODEN NOSE?
HE'S THE ONE WHO STOLE AWAY LITTLE GEORGIE!

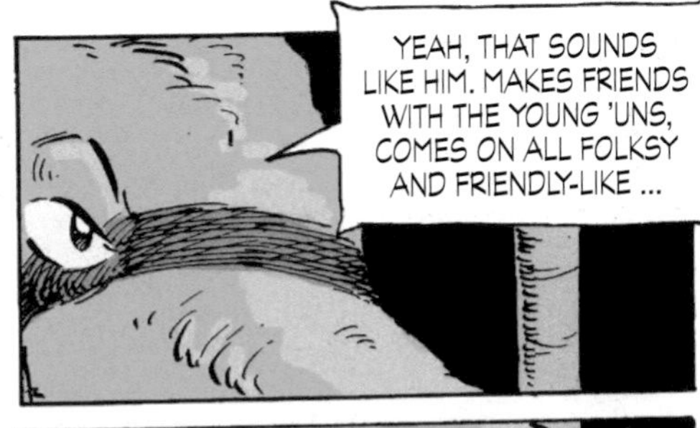
YEAH, THAT SOUNDS LIKE HIM. MAKES FRIENDS WITH THE YOUNG 'UNS, COMES ON ALL FOLKSY AND FRIENDLY-LIKE ...

THEN **WHAM**! YOU'RE IN A CRATE AND SHIPPED BACK HERE. PUT MOST OF US BEHIND BARS.

SO HE'S HERE? IN THE CITY?
NAW. MOVED ON. BUT IF YOU WANT HELP FINDING YOUR FRIEND ...

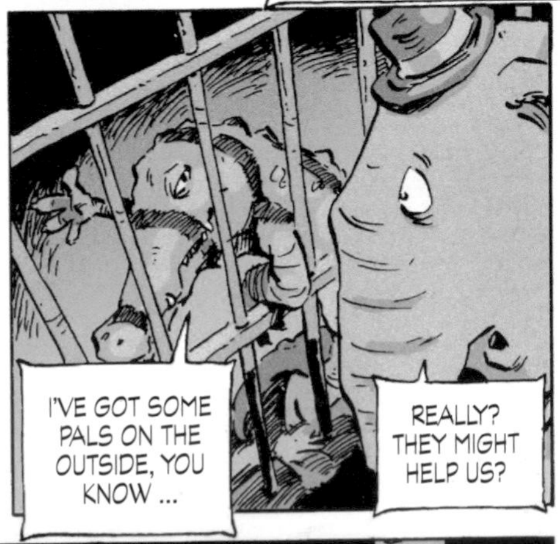
I'VE GOT SOME PALS ON THE OUTSIDE, YOU KNOW ...
REALLY? THEY MIGHT HELP US?

SURE. SURE THEY WOULD. HERE –

GO TO THIS ADDRESS. GIVE THEM THE ENVELOPE AND TELL THEM SMILING SAM SENT YOU.
13 Cayman Alley

CAYMAN ALLEY. THAT'S MILES FROM HERE! WE'LL HAVE TO CATCH A CAB.

TAXI!
WHOOSH!

ZOOM!
OH, TAXI!

SHEESH! IT'S NEVER LIKE THIS IN THE –
!
SCREECH!

CAUGHT ONE.
OTTO! WHAT ARE YOU DOING?!!

LEMME GO!
HE'S KINDA SMALL. SHOULD I THROW HIM BACK?

MY FRIEND AND I ARE IN NEED OF A LIFT, AND YOU LOOK AS IF YOU'RE IN NEED OF BEING DROPPED.
ALL RIGHT, ALREADY! GET IN.
THIS AIN'T GONNA WORK, PAL.
WAIT, I'VE GOT ANOTHER IDEA.

HOW COME EVERYWHERE I GO I GET TREATED LIKE BAGGAGE?
KLUNK!
SCREECH!
KLUNK!

SHORTLY AFTERWARD ...
CAYMAN ALLEY
SCREEECH!
KLUNK!
THIS IS AS FAR AS I GO, PALS.

THE ADDRESS YOU WANT IS DOWN THAT ALLEY.
THANKS. KEEP THE CHANGE!

GOOD LUCK! HAR! HAR!
I DIDN'T KNOW YOU HAD MONEY. WHERE'D YOU GET MONEY?
SCREECH!
KLUNK!
KLUNK-A-KLUNK!

I DIDN'T EVEN KNOW YOU HAD POCKETS ...
DROP IT, OTTO! LET'S GET MOVING. I'VE GOT A BAD FEELING ABOUT THIS PLACE.

IT MAKES MY FEATHERS MOLT. HERE WE GO, 13! GIVE THE DOOR A KNOCK, OTTO.
OKEY-DOKEY.
13

CRASH!
?!

I SAID A KNOCK! IS THAT A KNOCK?!

OHH, SO IT'S "BUST US OUT OF THE AIRPORT" OR "BASH US INTO THE ZOO"! BUT NOW IT'S "OOOO! PLEASE BE MORE CAREFUL" FROM MISTER PARROT POCKETS!
I SAID "DROP IT!!"

MON DIEU! KEEP EET DOWN! I'M TRYING TO SLEEP!

?!
YAWN!

THIS MUST BE THE GUY! GIVE HIM THE LETTER!
LETTER? OH, YEAH. UM, WE HAVE A LETTER FOR YOU. SMILING SAM SENT US.

EH? SMILING SAM? YOU KNOW SMILING SAM?

LET ME SEE ZEES LETTER.

HMMM! VEERY INTERESTING ...

IF YOU FOLLOW ME, PLEEZE.
AHEM!

AH, OUI! PERHAPS WE USE ZEE SERVICE ENTRANCE. ZEES WAY.
SO WHAT'S WITH THE BELT?

A SHORT WHILE LATER ...
DANGER KEEP OUT!
ALLIGATOR WRESTLING FEDERATION WORLD CHAMPION! THAT'S AMAZING!
WE'RE GOING IN THERE?
BUT OF COURSE!

YOU LIVE HERE?
OUI. EET'S VEERY NICE. WATERFRONT PROPERTY, QUIET. EXCEPT, OF COURSE, ZEE 'IP 'OP.
HIP HOP?

DON'T ASK.

SO YOU WERE REALLY WORLD CHAMPION?
OUI! PERHAPS YOU 'AVE 'EARD OF ME? CAJUN JOE?
DID YOU HAVE, LIKE, A SIGNATURE MOVE?
MAIS OUI! ZEE ATOMIC DEATH ROLL.
LIKE **ZEESE!** AHA!
SPLASH!
WOW.
TOUCHÉ.

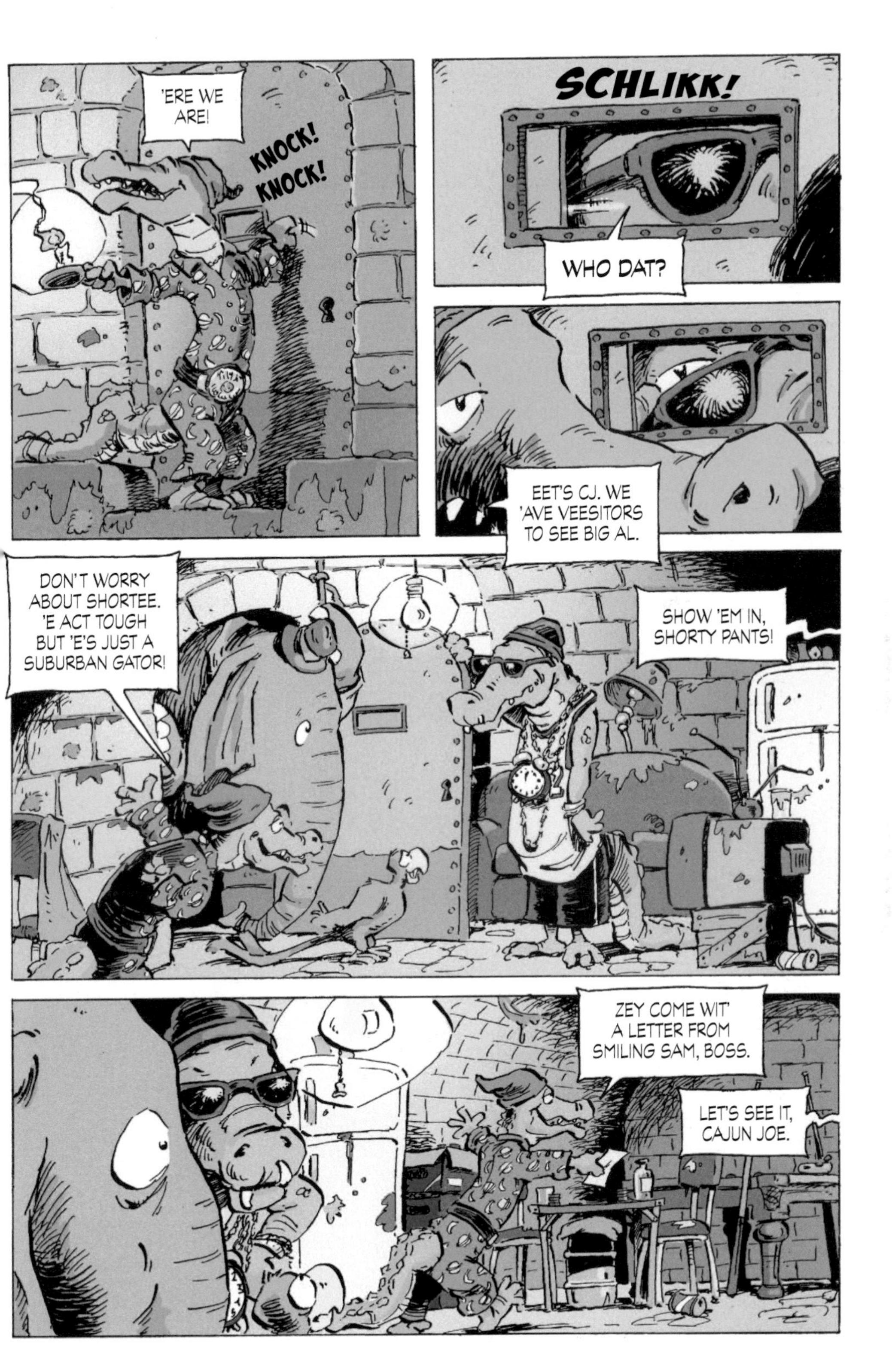
'ERE WE ARE!
KNOCK! KNOCK!
SCHLIKK!
WHO DAT?
EET'S CJ. WE 'AVE VEESITORS TO SEE BIG AL.
DON'T WORRY ABOUT SHORTEE. 'E ACT TOUGH BUT 'E'S JUST A SUBURBAN GATOR!
SHOW 'EM IN, SHORTY PANTS!
ZEY COME WIT' A LETTER FROM SMILING SAM, BOSS.
LET'S SEE IT, CAJUN JOE.

I T'OUGHT I MUST BRING ZEM 'ERE.
YA DONE GOOD, CJ.
HA!
Big Al,
I talked this simpleton and his birdbrained friend into smuggling out the plans for the Big House sewer system. Bust me out as soon as possible.
Cheers,
Smiling Sam
P.S. Bring lots of sacks!
DID YA LOOK AT DIS?
HE SAID YOU WOULD HELP MY FRIEND HERE FIND HIS PAL.
HE DID, DID HE? WELL, WE'RE KINDA BUSY RIGHT NOW. SO BEAT IT.
BUT HE PROMISED!

HERE, DUMBO, TAKE A PEANUT AND SHOVE OFF, WILL YA? SHORTY PANTS, SHOW OUR FRIENDS THE DOOR.
AH ... AH ...
?!
PLOINK!
AHH ...
??!

AH-CHOO!
MON DIEU!
WHAT THE – ?!
YO, SHOULD I THROW DA BUM OUT, BOSS?
HONK!
PEANUT ALLERGY.
NO, NO, WAIT! MAYBE I WAS A BIT HASTY ...
WE INTERRUPT THIS STORY TO BRING YOU AN IMPORTANT PUBLIC HEALTH ANNOUNCEMENT: WARNING! PEANUT ALLERGIES FOR HUMANS ARE SERIOUS! BUT PEANUT ALLERGIES FOR ELEPHANTS ARE FUNNY. BECAUSE ELEPHANTS LIKE PEANUTS, RIGHT? (IT'S IRONY. BUT I EXPECT YOU KNEW THAT.) WE NOW RETURN TO OUR STORY ...
I'M SURE WE CAN HELP FIND YOUR FRIEND. WE JUST HAVE TO DO A BIT OF SHOPPING FIRST, OKAY?

SOON AFTER ...
ALLIGARI BROS.
ALL KINDS OF CEMENT WORK
YO, I'M A MEAN INSTIGATA. I'M A BAD ALLIGATA.
BOOM-DE-BOOM-BOOM ...
OKAY, SO WE'RE ALL SET. YOU GOT THE BEANS, CAJUN JOE?
RIGHT 'ERE, BOSS!

YOU BOYS GOOD BACK THERE?
I'VE GOT A BAD FEELING ABOUT THESE GUYS, OTTO.
JUST A BIT OF SHOPPING, CRACKERS. THAT'S ALL. THEN WE GET GEORGIE!
HERE'S A LITTLE SUMPIN' AND I WON'T TELL YA AGAIN, I NEVER SHOULDA BEEN SPRUNG FROM THE ALLIGATA PEN.
24-7
BROS.
DS OF
T WORK
Milk $1.95 Qt

I DON'T LIKE WHAT'S GOING DOWN HERE, OTTO!
I GOTTA BIG SMILE BUT I'M MEAN INSIDE. SO RUN LIL' FISHY 'CAUSE YA NOWHERE TO HIDE.
!
'CAUSE I'M THE TYPE OF GATA WHO'S NOT SO DUMB. MESS WITH ME AN' I'LL BITE YO –
PAF!
TURN THAT CRUD OFF. TRY AND ACT PROFESSIONAL. SHEESH! IT'S NOT EVEN SINATRA!
?
THE KID'S BEEN BUSY.
BREAK-IN AT ZOO!
SUBWAY HERO
MYSTERY CRIME WAVE
COME 'ERE, OTTO. LET'S LOOK AT ZEE SNACKS.
MAYBE YOU LIKE SOME POTATO CHEEPS? CHOCOLATE BAR?
OR MAYBE SOME PEANUTS?!
INCOMING!

AH-CHOO!

AH-CHOO!
KA-CHING!
AH-CHOO!

R-R-R-RIINGG!
C'MON! LET'S SCRAM!

'CAUSE I'M A MEAN ALLIGATA, I'M AN INSTIGATA!
I TOLD YA, TURN THAT CRUD OFF!

ACROSS TOWN ...
THE ZOO? WHAT THE HECK WERE THEY DOING AT THE ZOO?!!
?!
JUST IN, BOSS. OUR BOYS BLEW UP A 24-7. AND THEY HAD HELP!
JEEZ! LOCAL OPERATIVES! LET'S GO!

BACK AT THE HIDEOUT ...
WHOOEE! SUCH A BEEG EXPLOSION!
MAN, YOU WAS SICK!
YES, WELL, JUST A PEANUT ALLERGY ACTUALLY.

WHAT A HAUL! GATOR JUICE ALL 'ROUND, BOYS!
GEE, I HAD NO IDEA SHOPPING WAS SO FUN.
GUMMY BEARS! TWINKIES! CARAMEL CORN – WHOOPS! NOT FOR YOU, BIG GUY! MAY CONTAIN PEANUTS!
OTTO,THAT WASN'T SHOPPING! IT WAS THEFT! AND THEY USED YOU –
OOO! SPICEY!
GIMME ANUDDER DEM GJ'S, DAWG!
NEW ORLEANS STYLE
WE'VE GOT TO GET OUT OF HERE, OTTO! THESE GUYS ARE TROUBLE.
YEAH, RIGHT, KID! REAL SOON!
TROUBLE? JEEZ, CRACKERS! THEY'RE GONNA HELP US FIND GEORGIE. RIGHT, GUYS?
SOMETHING'S NOT ADDING UP HERE. I WONDER WHAT WAS REALLY IN SMILING SAM'S LETTER?
YO, LIKE DIS, MAN.
NOW SHEEFT ZEE WEIGHT TO ZEE LEFT FOOT ...
WAIT! WHAT'S THERE IN THE WASTEPAPER BASKET?

I'M ALL GETTIN' FIZZY ON GATA JUICE
CHUG-A-LUG! CHUG-A-LUG!
IT'S SMILING SAM'S LETTER!
Gator Juice

SNAPPIN' TO THE BEAT FEELIN' REAL LOOSE!
CHUG-A-LUG! CHUG-A-LUG!
"BIRD-BRAINED"!

BEATIN' UP THE STREET IN MY GATA CAR ...
RIDIN' WITH MY CREW, TWINKIE IN MY CLAW!
FWIP!
YOU SHOULDN'T BE READING OTHER FOLKS' MAIL, BIRDY!
CHUG-A-LUG! CHUG-A-LUG!
GO, HOMIE!
I KNOW WHAT YOU'RE UP TO! OTTO, C'MON! WE'RE GETTING OUT OF HERE!
FERGETABOUTIT, BIRDY. LOOK AT 'IM. HE LIKES IT HERE. HE'S FORGOTTEN ALL ABOUT HIS LITTLE PAL, GEORGIE.

CHUG-A-LUG!
AND BY TOMORROW HE'LL HAVE FORGOTTEN ABOUT YOU!
NO! YOU DON'T KNOW OTTO! ELEPHANTS NEVER FOR –
SMACK!
UH!

CREAK!
SPLASH!

?!
MORNING SUN
SUSPECTS SOU

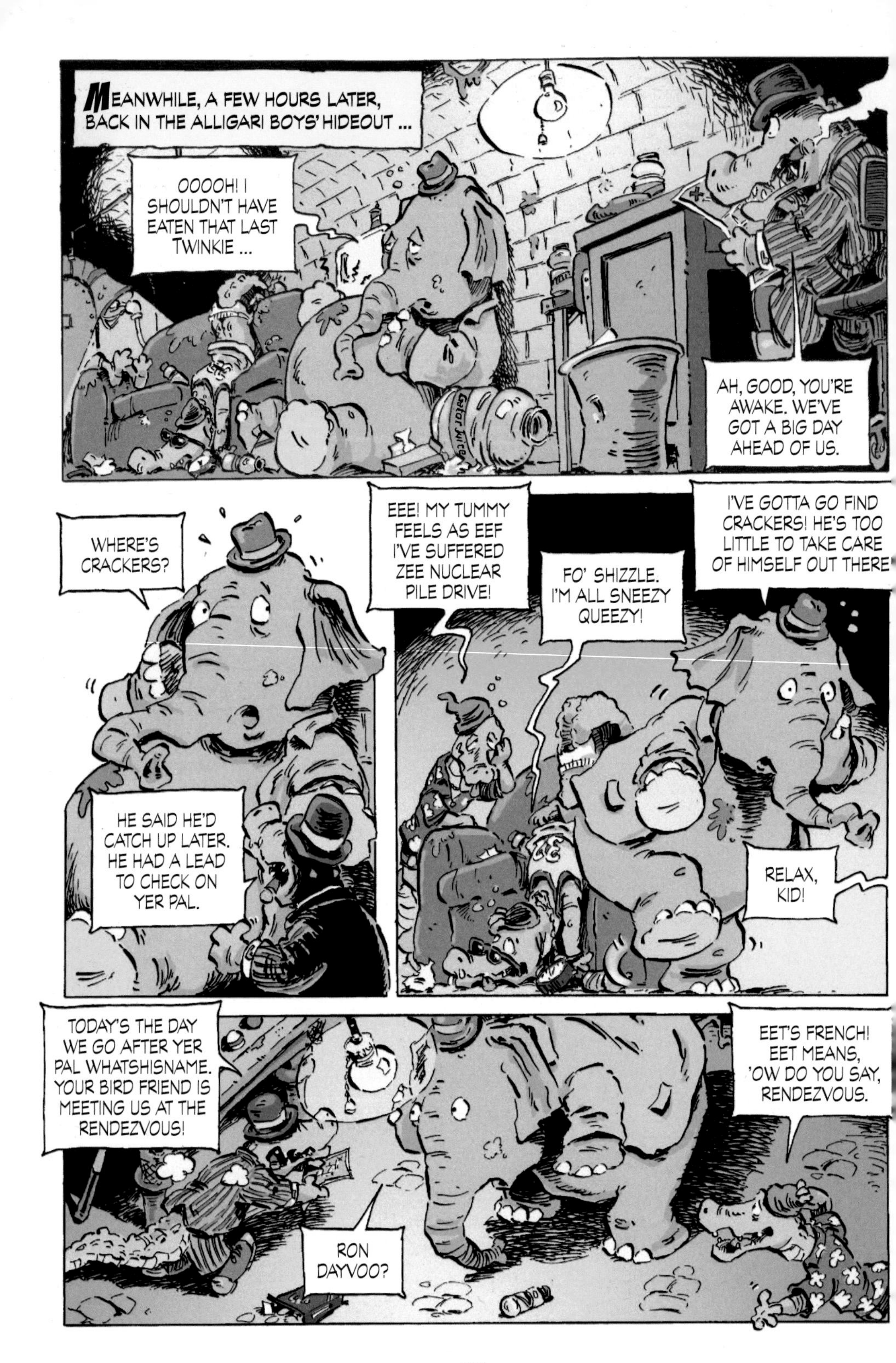
MEANWHILE, A FEW HOURS LATER, BACK IN THE ALLIGARI BOYS' HIDEOUT ...
OOOOH! I SHOULDN'T HAVE EATEN THAT LAST TWINKIE ...
AH, GOOD, YOU'RE AWAKE. WE'VE GOT A BIG DAY AHEAD OF US.
WHERE'S CRACKERS?
HE SAID HE'D CATCH UP LATER. HE HAD A LEAD TO CHECK ON YER PAL.
EEE! MY TUMMY FEELS AS EEF I'VE SUFFERED ZEE NUCLEAR PILE DRIVE!
FO' SHIZZLE. I'M ALL SNEEZY QUEEZY!
I'VE GOTTA GO FIND CRACKERS! HE'S TOO LITTLE TO TAKE CARE OF HIMSELF OUT THERE!
RELAX, KID!
TODAY'S THE DAY WE GO AFTER YER PAL WHATSHISNAME. YOUR BIRD FRIEND IS MEETING US AT THE RENDEZVOUS!
RON DAYVOO?
EET'S FRENCH! EET MEANS, 'OW DO YOU SAY, RENDEZVOUS.

EXACTLY! SO PULL YOURSELVES TOGETHER! WE'VE GOT A LONG DAY AHEAD OF US!

SEVERAL HOURS LATER ...
OHHHH!
RIGHT AT THE NEXT JUNCTION.
'ERE, 'AVE ANOTHER TWINKIE.
I NEVER SEEN DESE PIPES, BOSS. WHERE WE AT?

AND SEVERAL MORE HOURS LATER ...
OKAY, BOYS, THIS IS OUR STOP. CJ, SEE IF THE COAST IS CLEAR.
RIGHT, BOSS!

ALL CLEAR! I SEE NOBODEE!
OKAY, SHORTY PANTS, KID, LET'S GO.

SNIP! SNIP!

WAIT A MINUTE! THIS IS THE ZOO!
SSHHHHH!

BUT CRACKERS AND I ALREADY CHECKED HERE. NOBODY HAD HEARD OF GEORGIE.
YA JUST DIDN'T ASK THE RIGHT CROWD. NOW C'MON.
STAND HERE, KID. CAJUN JOE, YA GOT THE YOU-KNOW-WHATS?
RIGHT 'ERE, BOSS!
PEANUT?
?!
PLEASE DO NOT FEED THE ANIMALS
PLEASE DO NOT FEED THE ANIMALS
AH-CHOO!

NOW WHY'D YOU DO THAT?!
HELLO, BOYS. HELLO, OTTO.
?!
SAM! IT'S BEEN A LONG TIME!
TOO LONG, BOYS. I'M SICK OF THIS PRISON CHOW.
SO LET'S SCRAM, BOSS. YOUR SEWER MAP TAKES US RIGHT OUT OF HERE.
NOT SO FAST, BIG AL. DID YOU BRING THOSE SACKS?

WAZZUP?
EH? DID ANYONE HEAR A BIG KABOOM?
YEAH. MORE AN "AH-CHOO," REALLY.
TAKE A LOOK AT THESE MORONS. WITH THE HELP OF SNEEZY HERE, IT'S A SMORGASBORD!
WE CAN TAKE WHAT WE WANT AND COME BACK FOR MORE!

SNEEZY? SMORGASBORD? WHAT?! YOU'RE GONNA *EAT* THESE ANIMALS?
YOU BET, TUBBY. HMMM ... WHERE TO START?

HOW ABOUT A FEW OF THOSE LITTLE TASTIES AS APPETIZERS? BLOW THE CAGE, JUMBO.

FORGET IT! WHAT MAKES YOU THINK I'LL HELP YOU?
YOU'RE IN THICK WITH US NOW, OTTO. THERE'S NO GOING BACK.
CRACKERS WAS RIGHT! YOU'RE BAD GUYS. I'M NOT GONNA DO THIS!
!
CRACKERS, HUH? YOU'LL HELP IF YOU EVER WANNA SEE YOUR LITTLE PAL AGAIN.
GET HIM, BOYS!
32

AH-CHOO!
AH-CHOO!
AH-CHOO!

SNATCH 'EM UP, FELLAS!
I'LL TRADE YOU THIS ANGWANTIBO FOR YOUR PANDA.

OOWEE! OOWEE!
WHAT THE – ??
OOWEE! OOWEE! OOWEE!
MON DIEU!
RUN FOR IT, BOYS!
COPPERS!

POLICE! DROP THE KOALA AND PUT YOUR HANDS UP!
OTTO?
OTTO!
CRACKERS!
I CAME AS FAST AS I COULD!
THEY SAID YOU HAD LEFT, AND THEN THEY GAVE ME A PEANUT. AND YOU KNOW ME AND PEANUTS!
THEY'RE GETTING AWAY!

THE BAD GUYS ARE GETTING AWAY?!

C'MON, CRACKERS! I THINK I KNOW WHERE THEY'RE HEADED!

FASTER, CRACKERS! WE GOTTA STOP THEM!
WAIT! WE NEED A PLAN!

YOU TRIP THEM AND I'LL JUMP ON THEM!
NOW THAT'S A PLAN!

SHWOOOOP!

GEROMINO!

FWOOMP!
AND SO ...
... SO ONCE THEY FISHED ME OUT OF THE RIVER, I WAS ABLE TO FILL THEM IN ON WHAT THE ALLIGARI BOYS WERE UP TO.
HE SANG LIKE A CANARY.
HEE HEE!
A CANARY?
WHAT A MOVE! BETTER THAN ZEE ATOMIC DEATH ROLL! BAM!
SHADDUP!

JUST A MINUTE ...
I REALLY THOUGHT WE WERE PALS.
SORRY, OTTO DAWG.
WE WERE, KID. ZEE PEANUT STUFF ... JUST BEEZNESS.
WELL, I DON'T THINK FRIENDS ACT THAT WAY. YOU PROMISED TO HELP ME FIND GEORGIE.
AH, OUI, ABOUT YOUR PAL ... I DON' T'INK 'E WAS EVER IN ZEESE CITY.
WHAT?
I T'INK I SEE 'IM YEARS AGO. DOWN IN ZEE BAYOU, WHEN I WAS GATOR WRESTLING. LEETLE CUTIE, RIGHT?
YEAH, REAL CUTE!
'E WAS OUTSIDE MY AGENT'S OFFICE ONE DAY, 'IM AN' A MAN WIT' A WOODEN NOSE, WAITING TO GO IN.
THAT'S HIM! THAT'S GEORGIE! WHERE'D HE GO?
SORRY, KID. DAT'S ALL I KNOW.
CRACKERS! CAJUN JOE SAW GEORGIE! IN A BAYOO!

SO WE'RE GOOD TO GO?
YEP. YOUR STORY CHECKS OUT. AND WE'VE BEEN TRYING TO BAG THE ALLIGARI BOYS FOR YEARS.
THERE WERE RUMORS THAT THEY MAY BE HIDING OUT IN THE SEWERS ...
YEP. THANKS TO YOU TWO, ANOTHER URBAN MYTH BUSTED.
STOP IT. YOU'RE KILLIN' ME.
I JUST DON'T WANT TO SEE YOU BOYS SHOWING UP ON ANY MORE SURVEILLANCE SCREENS. KEEP YOUR NOSE ... ER, BEAK ... ER, TRUNK CLEAN, OKAY?
DON'T WORRY. THERE'S SOMEONE WE'VE GOT TO TRACK DOWN. AND IT SOUNDS LIKE WE'RE NOT GOING TO FIND HIM IN THIS CITY.
BAYOU, HUH, OTTO? SO YOU DIDN'T FORGET YOUR OLD CHUM?
NOPE. AND I DIDN'T FORGET YOU, EITHER, LITTLE PAL.
THE END

FOR LISA, WHO NEVER OUTGREW COMIC BOOKS

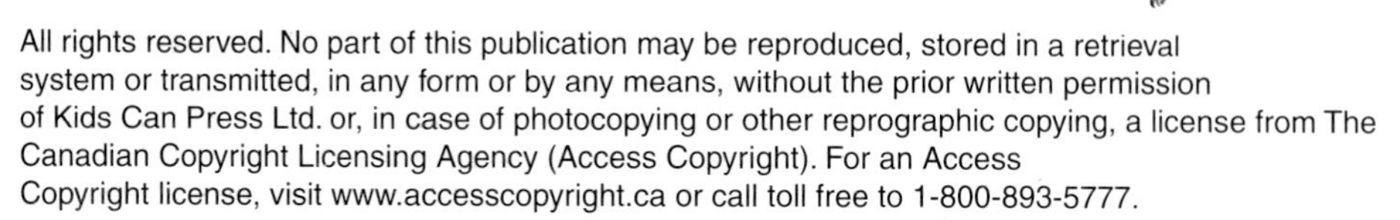

Kids Can Press acknowledges the financial support of the Government of Ontario, through the Ontario Media Development Corporation's Ontario Book Initiative; the Ontario Arts Council; the Canada Council for the Arts; and the Government of Canada, through the BPIDP, for our publishing activity.

Published in Canada by
Kids Can Press Ltd.
25 Dockside Drive
Toronto, ON M5A 0B5

Published in the U.S. by
Kids Can Press Ltd.
2250 Military Road
Tonawanda, NY 14150

www.kidscanpress.com

The artwork in this book was rendered in pen and ink line and colored in Photoshop.
The text is set in Graphite Std Narrow and BadaBoom Pro BB.

Edited by Tara Walker
Designed by Bill Slavin and Marie Bartholomew

The hardcover edition of this book is smyth sewn casebound.
The paperback edition of this book is limp sewn with a drawn-on cover.
Manufactured in Buji, Shenzhen, China, in 4/2011 by WKT Company

CM 11 0 9 8 7 6 5 4 3 2 1
CM PA 11 0 9 8 7 6 5 4 3 2 1

Library and Archives Canada Cataloguing in Publication

Slavin, Bill
Big city Otto / written by Bill Slavin with Esperança Melo ; illustrated by Bill Slavin.

(Elephants never forget ; 1)
Includes index.
ISBN 978-1-55453-476-0 (bound). ISBN 978-1-55453-477-7 (pbk.)

I. Melo, Esperança II. Title. III. Series: Slavin, Bill. Elephants never forget ; 1.

PS8587.L43B54 2011   jC813'.54   C2011-900761-4

Kids Can Press is a Corus™ Entertainment company